W9-APD-182

For Sonny Mac Cooper

E
461-9808

A LION

First U.S. edition 2018

Library of Congress Catalog Card Number pending
ISBN 978-0-7636-9731-0

18 19 20 21 22 23 TLF 10 9 8 7 6 5 4 3 2 1

Printed in Dongguan, Guangdong, China

This book was typeset in Cochin.
The illustrations were done in ink and paint
and rendered digitally.

Candlewick Press
99 Dover Street
Somerville, Massachusetts 02144

visit us at www.candlewick.com

IS A LION

Polly Dunbar

CANDLEWICK PRESS

This is a lion.

Fierce, isn't he?
Too fierce for you?

Well . . .

Is a lion
still a lion if . . .

he wears a hat?

And is a lion
still a lion if . . .

he carries
an umbrella,
too?

Is a lion still a lion if . . . he skips down

the street singing *"Hoobie-doobie-doo"*?

And then . . .

he hangs up his hat (his umbrella, too),

and asks, "How *IS* your auntie Sue?"

Is a lion still a lion if . . .

after the usual "How

do

you

dos?"

and "How do you don'ts!"

he says, "May I have this dance?"

And *hoobie-doobie* dances you . . .

all . . .

around . . .

the room!

Weeeeee

Is a lion still a lion if he says . . .

"Oh, yes, lunch
would be lovely,
thank you."

And he eats all of his greens . . .

and his plate, too!
Till it's gobble,
gobble,
gone!

"And NOW I'd like some pudding . . .

PLEASE?"

Is a lion still a lion if . . .

his eyes are bright,
and his teeth
oh-so-pearly-white,
and he looks like

he might just . . .

BITE!

YES!

A LION
IS A LION
IS A LION!

And now it's time to

GO! GO! GO!

OR . . .

is it time to simply say . . .

"No!"

"No! No! No! NO!

You may NOT have pudding,
please!

Lunch was NOT lovely,
thank you!

You may NOT have this
hoobie-doobie dance.

NO WAY!

You may *NOT* hang up
your hat or wipe your feet.

You can take your umbrella, too!
And never mind Aunt Sue!

No, you may *NOT*
come in —

we *DO* mind if you do!"

BANG
SLAM

You
shut
that
door . . .

and watch him go —
lickety-split — down the street.

PHEW!

So, please remember,
A LION IS *ALWAYS* A LION!

And do you think he'd
like to eat you, too?
(Till you're gobble,
gobble, gone?)

"Mmmm . . .
Don't mind
if I do."

No, no, no, Lion!

You may *NOT*!

NOW...*SHOOO*!